DIRTY
This ~~Little Tiger~~ book belongs to:

_____

_____

_____

_____

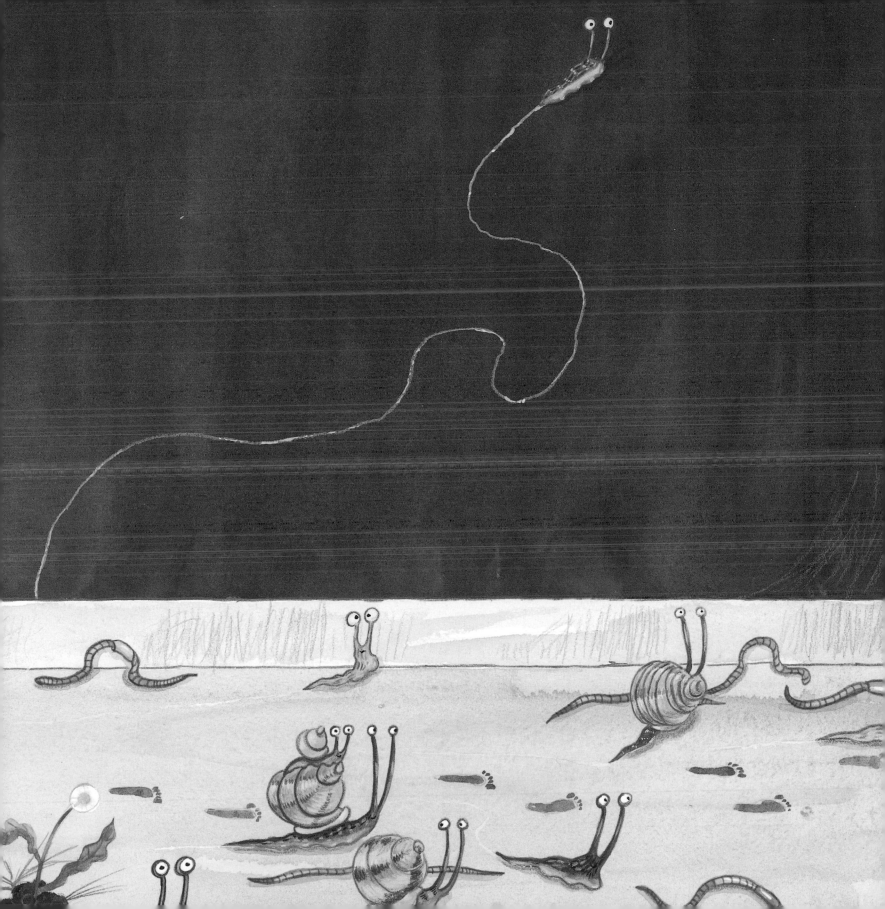

for Julia

LITTLE TIGER PRESS
An imprint of Magi Publications
1 The Coda Centre, 189 Munster Road, London SW6 6AW
www.littletigerpress.com

First published in Great Britain 2002
This edition published 2003

Text and illustrations copyright © David Roberts 2002
David Roberts has asserted his right to be identified as the author and illustrator
of this work under the Copyright, Designs and Patents Act, 1988
All rights reserved

ISBN 978-1-85430-820-7

A CIP catalogue record for this book is available
from the British Library

Printed in Belgium by Proost

DIRTY BERTIE

David Roberts

LITTLE TIGER PRESS
London

This is Bertie.
He used to have dirty habits.

If Bertie saw a sweet on the floor,
he would pick it up and eat it.

But Bertie's mum would shout …

"NO, BERTIE! THAT'S DIRTY, BERTIE!"

If Bertie had a bogey up his nose,
he'd try to pick it out.

But Bertie's dad would shout …

"NO, BERTIE! THAT'S DIRTY, BERTIE!"

Bertie liked to go hunting for
slugs and worms in the garden,
and play with them.

But Bertie's big sister, Suzy, would shout …

"NO, BERTIE! THAT'S DIRTY, BERTIE!"

Sometimes, Bertie's dog would lick his face,
so Bertie would lick him back.

But Bertie's gran would shout ...

"NO, BERTIE! THAT'S DIRTY, BERTIE!"

If Bertie saw his cat do a wee on the flowerbed,
Bertie would do a wee on the flowerbed too.

But everyone would shout ...

"NO, BERTIE! THAT'S DIRTY, BERTIE!"

Bertie soon learned not to ...

wee in the flowerbed ...

or play with slugs and worms ...

or eat sweets off the floor ...

or even lick the dog's face.

bleugh!

But there is one dirty habit that
Bertie cannot stop!

When no one is looking,
he still picks bogeys
out of his nose ...

and sometimes...

he eats them!

UGH!

More great books for messy monsters!

Oodles of Noodles
Diana Hendry Illustrated by Sarah Massini

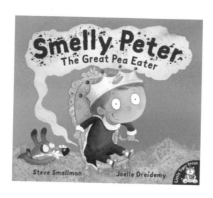
Smelly Peter
The Great Pea Eater
Steve Smallman Joelle Dreidemy

The Three Horrid Pigs
and the Big Friendly Wolf
by Liz Pichon

SUPER SPUD AND THE Stinky Space Rescue!
SAM LLOYD BEN CORT

POOH! IS THAT YOU, BERTIE?
David Roberts

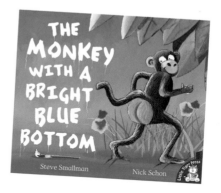
THE MONKEY WITH A BRIGHT BLUE BOTTOM
Steve Smallman Nick Schon

For information regarding any of the above titles or for our catalogue, please contact:
Little Tiger Press, 1 The Coda Centre, 189 Munster Road, London SW6 6AW, UK
Tel: 020 7385 6333 Fax: 020 7385 7333
e-mail: info@littletiger.co.uk
www.littletigerpress.com